Shoe-la-la!

la-la!

by **Karen Beaumont**

illustrated by **LeUyen Pham**

SCHOLASTIC INC.
New York Toronto London Auckland
Sydney Mexico City New Delhi Hong Kong

Party dresses, party hair . . .
Need new party shoes to wear.
Emily, Ashley, Kaitlyn, Claire!
Let's go find the perfect pair!

Shoe-la-la

You're Invited!

Shoe-la-la!

They're *everywhere.*

Rows and rows!
These or those?
Up, up on our tippy toes.
Can't wait to choose new shoes.
Here goes!

Shoes with zippers,

 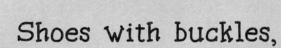

Shoes with straps,

 Shoes with buckles,

Shoes with taps.

 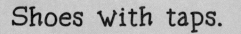

Shoes with laces, shoes with bows,

Sorry, sir. We *don't* like those. They hurt our toes.

I'll try on this rainbow pair.

Hey! These match my underwear!

Lots and lots of leopard spots.

Pink and purple polka dots.

These show off
my pretty feet.

These look good
enough to eat.

Fuzzy boots for
when it snows.

Ballerina
on my toes!

Cowgirl . . .

Rock star . . .

Princess . . .

Bride . . .

This pair? That pair? Can't decide.

Fancy ribbons,
    Frilly lace.
Shoe-la-la!
    We *love* this place!

Sparkly diamonds, pretty pearls,
Ritzy, glitzy

Glamour Girls!

Uh-oh!
Store's about to close!
Which shoes
should we choose—
who knows?

Emily,
Ashley,
Kaitlyn,
Claire!
Hurry, hurry!
Pick a pair!

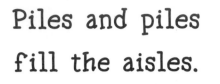

Piles and piles
fill the aisles.

Never seen
so many styles.

Shop and shop until we drop!
Guess it's time for us to STOP!

Eeny, meeny, my oh my!
Just don't know which shoes to buy.

Can't decide. We've seen too many.

Sorry, sir.
We *don't* want ANY!

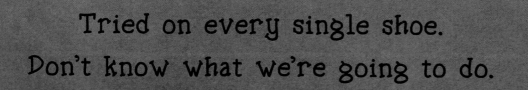

Tried on every single shoe.
Don't know what we're going to do.

Party dresses,

Party hair . . .

Perfect party shoes to wear!

For my daughters, Christina and Nicolyn.
I love you with all of my heart . . . and "sole"!
—K.B.

To Kay, the ultimate Shoe-Gal.
—L.P.

ISBN 978-0-545-39465-9

Text copyright © 2011 by Karen Beaumont.
Illustrations copyright © 2011 by LeUyen Pham.
All rights reserved. Published by Scholastic Inc.
SCHOLASTIC and associated logos are trademarks and/or
registered trademarks of Scholastic Inc.

12 11 10 9 8 7 6 5 4 3 2   12 13 14 15 16/0

Printed in the U.S.A.   40

First Scholastic paperback printing, September 2011

The text was set in Spellstone.
Book design by Lillie Howard